LITTLE LABYRINTHS

ALSO BY SEAN WILLIAMS

<u>Series</u>

The Books of the Change

The Books of the Cataclysm

The Broken Land

Astropolis

Twinmaker

The Fixers

Star Wars: The Force Unleashed

Troubletwisters (with Garth Nix)

Have Sword, Will Travel (with Garth Nix)

Evergence (with Shane Dix)

Orphans (with Shane Dix)

Geodesica (with Shane Dix)

Star Wars: New Jedi Order: Force Heretic (with Shane Dix)

<u>Standalone novels</u>

Metal Fatigue

The Resurrected Man

Her Perilous Mansion

Spirit Animals: Blood Ties (with Garth Nix)

Star Wars: The Old Republic: Fatal Alliance

LITTLE LABYRINTHS

SPECULATIVE MICROFICTIONS

SEAN WILLIAMS

Brain Jar Press
PO Box 6687
Upper Mt Gravatt, QLD, 4122
Australia
www.BrainJarPress.com

Cover design by Brain Jar Press
Cover Image: The Truth is Somewher Near, Dennis Svitkin/Shutterstock

ISBN: 978-1-922479-15-0 (Ebook) | 978-1-922479-14-3 (Paperback)

CONTENTS

UBER

"Hop in, mate."

I double-checked the app. My driver was supposedly "Edward" in a white Camry. His photo matched, but if the car had ever been white, it wasn't now. Down the passenger side trailed what looked like giant claw marks.

"Seriously?"

"Just superficial. Tom, is it?"

It seemed wrong to send him packing, and besides, that would hurt my ranking.

The interior of the car was little better than the exterior, smelling of molten plastic and covered in what looked suspiciously like ash.

"Forgive the mess, mate. Been a bad day."

Edward looked oddly familiar, but I couldn't place him. He was bearded, weathered, and dressed in camo gear.

"Cosplay?" I ventured. *Fury Road*, perhaps.

Edward grinned. He was missing a tooth. "I know what that is. Drove a bunch home from Comic-Con last month. They were a riot."

We pulled away from the curb, the screen on Edward's app guiding him through the suburban streets, heading for the city. His phone was a model I didn't recognize, with a crack right across its face.

"You haven't figured it out yet," Edward said, looking at me sideways as he drove.

"If it's not cosplay, you've had a really bad day."

"A bad life, mate," he said. "But that's not what I'm talking about. Where you've seen me before."

I turned to face him front on. "How… ?"

"You'll know how when you know why. As to the car… well, people like me, we come from the edges, where it's thin. Reality, I mean. Some of us go back and forth, world to world. It's not as hard as you think…"

He took a corner and I took a hard look at him. Edward seemed the kind of guy who might catch, kill, and clean an animal with his bare hands but wouldn't waste time burdening a stranger with his brand of crazy.

"You're having me on."

"Nah. You'll see us everywhere, now you know to look. Beggars. Streetwalkers. Lunatics. Survivalists. All types."

"Doing… what?"

"Well, I'm one of the lucky ones. Got a car, so I can work. Plenty less fortunate…"

He shrugged expressively, and I decided to play along.

"That would explain missing people. They go too close to the edges and… what, fall off?"

"More like stepping through honey. Yeah, I guess it might explain a few. But the traffic is mainly one way. Believe me, no one would willingly go where I come from. It's the same for most. If you're not careful, you end up in one of the really shithouse universes."

I thought of our collapsing environment and recent political troubles. "This isn't one of them?"

"Land of milk and honey! And doesn't the government know it, calling us freeloaders, job-stealers, terrorists, whatever. But the way we see it, you need us just as much as we need you. Those of us with families and friends back home are desperate. We'll do anything."

Right, I thought. *Activism plus a captive audience of one.* Cute. Better than passing the time chatting about kids that might be imaginary, or in obstinate silence, I guessed.

"I don't want to argue with you," I said, "but what about disease? Isn't that a concern?"

"Yeah, well, there have been some fuck-ups. Would you personally slam the door on a parallel Earth full of people dying from AIDS, though? When the bug's probably going to leak through anyway? When the cure might be over here in your science—or in your genes? The smart fellow's share is on every dish, as my Daddo used to say."

If he was trying to get a reaction, he succeeded.

"*What* did you say?"

"You heard me."

"That proverb... my grandfather used to say it, too."

"And you couldn't say '*daideó*' either, could you? So you called him Daddo instead. Weird, huh?"

I looked at him again, and this time really *looked* at him, through the beard, and the tan, and the scars...

"It's impossible. The app says 'Edward'."

"Fake ID, mate, or else I'd be out on my ear."

"But you're..."

"You, yes."

"From a..."

"Parallel world. Saw our name and face pop up in the app and I thought, why not?"

"You're not going to..."

"Kill you and take over your life? Hardly worth the bother. I'd inevitably slip up, and then I'd be in a whole world of trouble. And in return, you won't turn me in?"

"No, of course I won't." That would be impossible, morally and practically. I had deadlines to meet, and the process of calling the dogs on one's hard-done-by twin would undoubtedly take more than a phone call to immigration.

"What... happened? I mean, how did you... I... become you?"

Edward-the-alternate-Tom waved philosophically with his left hand, a gesture I too made when words were inadequate. "Hot war in the Middle East, 1986. Nasty. We don't think about it much anymore. Got bigger things to worry about."

"Is there anything I can do?"

"You'll figure it out. Oh hey, we're here. Nice joint."

The car pulled to a halt. Work's façade seemed particularly hollow this morning as I considered the lot of my other self and people like him. If my reality really wasn't as terrible here as everyone seemed to think, I swore to be more appreciative, and kinder to those less fortunate.

"It's been... something," I said, holding out my hand.

"You said it, mate. Take it easy."

The battered old Camry drove off up the street, and I remembered my question. My obligation.

I reached into my pocket and pulled out my phone. There was his face—*my* face, old before its time—under the *Ride Complete* banner.

I tapped the screen.

Five stars.

THE MISADVENTURES OF TOM JONES, TIME TRAVELLER

Being a dialogue between two hemispheres of the author's brain
that is neither uncommon nor blessed with a happy outcome

Wow.

Best. Dream. Ever.

Are you getting it down?

It practically writes itself! Beloved literary hero in an adventure leaping between epochs instead of bedrooms...

Don't forget the bit where Tom vanishes from Molly's arms and lands naked on the Western front. That's hot.

... a picaresque bildungsroman the like of which has never been seen...

Time travel with titillation is what it is.

Don't be vulgar.

He jumps a century every time he comes. It's so vulgar it's brilliant!

It's a metaphor for generational memory and youth's misspent passions, taking the grandest themes of Fielding and Wells and—

Mashing them together in a story that made you sweaty. Don't deny it. I was there.

Yes, but that's not the point—

We want it to sell, don't we? That is the point.

We still want it to be about something! Something more than the crap you're always filling our head with.

Here we go. You always look down on the stories I like. So what if they sometimes have spaceships in them! Not my fault if all you see in them is giant space cigars.

Everything's a metaphor—

For what? The overreach of the Jacobite Revolution? Yeah, sure. This is just like the time you convinced me that teleporters deconstruct contemporary notions of identity and embodiment.

They do, and I still maintain we had a perfectly good story until you added all that violence. Attract the male audience, you said. Help it sell, you said. And did it?

No, but—

Exactly. We're never going to sell anything at the rate we're going.

Not if you keep sucking the life out of every idea we ever have.

Not if you keep dragging everything down into the gutter.

Philistine.

Ignoramus.

God, this is exhausting.

The argument or because it's three in the morning and we drank too much tequila again?

We take the fifth.

Ha. Let's sleep on it, then, see what we've got in the morning. Maybe this time we'll figure it out.

Deal. Goodnight.

Sweet dreams.

Seriously?

TEARS OF THE LIVING DEAD

In the gutted supermarket we have been using as a temporary shelter I catch Valerie wiping at her cheeks.

"Is that... ?"

"Nothing," she says, guiltily.

But it is too late. I pull away from her and slip my gun from its holster with terrible ease.

"Wait." She backs up against a shelf that once held tinned food, making it rattle.

I joined her a month ago, finding strength and sanity in the company of another woman. We understand what happened better than men do, I think. But recently, I've caught her sneaking out at night in the hope of finding... *hope*, I guess. Signs of recovery among the herds of weakening ill, resistance in the next generation, I don't know. I admire her even as I despair at her recklessness. Hasn't the mothering instinct gotten enough people killed already? Has Valerie forgotten that the virus hides in the most innocent and tragic of places, unsuspected by anyone until far too late?

"I honestly thought it was called the Reaping," she said when we first met. "My preacher had a speech impediment."

When I close my eyes I see my ten-year-old boy, tears

streaming down his cheeks, as the thing he has become rips at my face in order to get at the pituitary gland he so badly craves.

"Can't we grieve?" Valerie says now. "Even after all we've been through?"

I thought she understood.

"You can grieve all you want. Just don't cry about it."

It's the one rule left, since the Weeping.

I shoot Valerie between the eyes to make absolutely sure.

THE GOGGLE

The moon. The city. A street.

"Look, Mummy! It's a Goggle!"

"That's 'gargoyle', darling." The woman tugged on the boy's hand, pulling him after her toward the lighted windows at the end of the street. "And don't point. It's only the moon that makes it look like it's moving."

"But — "

"No buts. We were supposed to be home from Aunt May's an hour ago."

The boy allowed himself to be led away, twisting his upper body in order to watch the gnarled silhouette as it moved slowly across the roof. Its shoulders were hunched, its limbs twisted but strong; its neck was thick and brutish. The distended bumps on either side of its head might have been horns or grotesquely deformed ears. The shadow it made against the sky looked like a living piece of the city, impossible to tell from a chimney or a cornice, except that it did appear to be moving.

"The Goggle," whispered the boy, fascinated by the sight. "It's so close!"

This time his mother said nothing, just tightened her grip on his hand and hurried them home.

. . .

When woman and child had passed, the gargoyle dropped heavily onto the sidewalk. Crossing the street with leaden footsteps, it scuffled to where they had trod and stooped to inspect the pavement. Something in its wide, moss-stained forehead clicked and whirred. It scratched its ear in puzzlement, and went to follow.

Another larger gargoyle stepped out of the shadows on the other side of the road, and hurried — inasmuch as it was able to — to stop the first in its tracks.

"What are you doing?" it asked with some urgency.

"Pebbles," said the first in a voice like a sarcophagus sliding over concrete. It pointed along the street to where the boy and his mother had gone. "Went that way. Pebbles!"

"That's 'people', darling," said the larger gargoyle, its malformed face softening slightly. "And you shouldn't follow them. It only encourages them to point."

"But —"

"No buts." Taking the first gargoyle by the arm, the larger moved back across the street. "We haven't got all night, you know."

The gargoyle allowed itself to be led away, swivelling its upper body in order to stare at the pool of light at the end of the street: bright, strange and soft, it was, like the creatures that lit the lights. As fleeting, too. It had seen such things before, on occasions, but still hadn't determined whether they were animals or plants. Barely did they appear before they were gone again.

"Pebbles," it whispered, stone teeth grating on the sibilant. "So far away..."

The larger gargoyle just tugged it back up onto the roof, and nodded.

THE EMPIRE'S SON

The cliff face is icy and black, and Andrew Irvine is falling, albeit slowly. He can no longer feel his fingers, but he knows that gravity hasn't completely seized him yet. If it had, he would already be dead—like poor George, who had to be cut free, the first Englishman to stand on the summit just weight to be discarded lest he bring Sandy down too.

The so-called "holy" mountain has claimed them both now.

"Come on, Sandy," he tells the wind. It won't do to give in. What would Lyn think? The letter in which she wrote so powerfully about the importance of wishes is tucked under his gabardine. He wishes he could read it now, but it's too dark and his hands... the slow business of falling...

Golden light strikes his face, startling him out of a warm fog. Has one of the others come? Charles, perhaps? Good old Charles.

But the two lamps look like nothing so much as those of a Railless trolleybus, and the Himalayan cliff face a road in England, against which he is spreadeagled like a man already dead.

Andrew Irvine, this Empire's son, lets go.

THE TRILERBE DULCIFTIFY

Time is cut, psated.

An ernicepexed toerampl tellvater kowns taht, as lnog as the bingening and the end of oen's jureony rimean the smae as tehy wree, it denos't mettar waht canghes ocucr in the mildde. Railtey siltl snacs. It's a bit lkie qutunam faom: annithyg geos peovdrid all the vurital piraclets sanp bcak in the box wehn the Pclank innastt is oevr. The dulciftify, of cruose, leis in minkag srue one deson't waerk hovac, and snepd the rset of oen's lfie tynrig to put it bcak teteghor aigan.

Psated, cut.

Life goes on, all the better for not knowing.

SEEKING THE GREAT CURRENT
BY MATTHEW CROPLEY & SEAN WILLIAMS

"You're going the wrong way!" The ghost of the dead girl stamps the boat's deck.

With long, measured strokes, the morguist pulls the oars, taking solace in the gentle splash sparkle of the moonlit ocean. An S-shaped hook in brass, pointed at the tip, swings like a pendulum from a thong around his neck. He breathes deeply of the salty air, ignoring the sickly-sweet scent of rot and the ache of his ageing muscles.

Another dead girl, a long time ago, lies heavily on his thoughts.

The ghost of this dead girl refuses to look at her body. But then, of course, she does look. They always do. It's stiff and curled in on itself, eyes open, staring up at the moon. Her face is blank and pale, her rough-woven shift stained black. A shell necklace is knotted in her hair. Blue veins, darker than the unfinished tattoos around her ears, extend from the bite mark in her neck down to her collarbone.

"You have to take me home," the girl insists, her hollow voice echoing across the water. "I must be shriven in order to rejoin the Great Current or... oh! Why aren't you listening to me?"

He peers up at her from under his sealskin hood. The lamp sways on its hook and its orange glow makes him squint.

"Be patient," he croaks.

The dead girl clutches at an oar, hoping to break his implacable stroke, but though she strains with all her ethereal might, the oar sweeps on unhindered.

She stumbles to her knees and finds herself momentarily staring across inky water back the way they have come. There, her island home of Batua forms a dark blotch on the horizon. Tiny orange lights twinkle across the ocean around the bay. The lamps of the fishing fleet, flickering through spritsails furled for the night.

Part of her stretches thinner with every tug on his oars.

"If you don't take me back," she whispers, "I'll be stuck like this forever."

"True enough," he says, angling the boat towards the gap between two small jungle islets several boat lengths ahead.

"Don't you care?" The translucent shade of the dead girl on the deck leaps back to her feet. "Mother will be wondering why I'm not back. She'll be worried sick. She needs to know what happened to me—"

"Don't tell me what she needs, girl," he growls, low and deep.

"But who are you?" she asks, her voice reaching a frantic high note. "You spirit me away in your boat, you refuse to tell me anything, you're not one of us or you would never—"

A hoot erupts from the night, and a rotten mango passes through the girl, exploding against the deck in a shower of sickly-sweet muck. The girl turns in shock. They're passing between the two jungle islets. On branches of a palm tree hanging over the water sits another ghost. Only vaguely human, features worn smooth by time, it hoots at her with words crude but almost recognisable. Time makes them stronger, even as it robs them of who they were.

More ghosts emerge from the trees to throw fruit, dirt, branches at their newest brethren. Their cries form an enraged clamour.

"Row faster!" the girl screams. A branch hits her corpse, twisting its arm, and she tries to shield it, but the next missile passes through her too and gouges a bloody furrow into the skin of what was once her face.

A clump of dirt hits the morguist's oilskin cloak and slides away.

"I've never seen ghosts so strong. They must be ancient," the girl says as the boat leaves the islets and their rowdy denizens behind. She stands, shaken, eyes wide and pale. "I don't want to become like that. Please, take me back to Batua to be shriven. At least drop me on a fishing boat or something."

"After."

"After? After what?"

The man points to the girl's corpse, now covered in a web of blue veins that glistens wetly against moonlight pale skin.

The girl gags.

"I was... I was collecting cockles for dinner on the West Shore... Something small, like a bug, came out of the shifting sand. It bit me."

"Ghargun larva."

"What's a ghargun larva?"

The man cocks his head, listening to the lapping of the seawater against the hull.

"You'll see soon enough."

"Why won't you just tell me?"

He pulls on the left oar, changing course slightly.

"When a ghargun spawns," he says, "the larvae swim out to look for fish. What a larva can't find in the water, it'll look for on land, and since your folk have fished too much around these parts, well... You were unlucky, and I'm sorry it happened to you, but it ain't the ghargun's fault. Just doin' what's natural."

The man draws in the oars and rises, rolling his shoulders to work out the stiffness of the rowing and the weight he's been carrying for so long.

Then he stands and moves to the body.

Under the skin, the distended veins, shapes move and shift.

The girl screams, stumbling backwards onto the deck.

"What is that?" the dead girl screeches.

"Baby ghargun," he says as he lifts the body into his arms with a grunt. It shifts wetly as the skin stretches and contorts, a dozen tiny shapes trying to break through.

"Kill them!" the girl yells.

The man drops the corpse overboard. As it hits the water it bursts, skin tearing like the thinnest rice paper. Tiny shapes stream out, shiny carapaces catching the moonlight as they thrash in the water. A chorus of high-pitched clicking sounds out above their fevered splashing.

The girl stares overboard, her mouth open in revulsion and horror. Her body floats facedown, torn open, ravaged by the creatures that bred, fed and grew inside her. "Are you drowning them? Is that why you wouldn't take me home? Get my body back, quickly! It's not too late!"

The man holds a hand up to her. "Wait."

The boat tips as a thump reverberates through its hull. The girl stumbles, but the man just sways with the movement.

Three deep clicks like blocks of coral rapping against one another vibrate through the ocean.

The morguist unships one of the oars and taps three times on the bottom of the hull.

Question. Reply.

A gigantic mass surfaces next to the boat, raising up a wave that streams off the man's oilskin cloak and passes entirely through the girl's ethereal body. The boat rocks but does not tip. Heavily segmented, five times as big as a hut, the creature's carapace catches the moonlight in gleaming waves.

The clicking, both high and low, intensifies as tendrils streak out from beneath the water to caress the baby ghargun, drawing them close.

The girl watches, shocked and awed into silence.

"Their mother," supplies the morguist.

The huge creature rolls in the water to regard the man with a multi-faceted eye as big as the boat. They stare at each other for a moment that seems long for the man but, he suspects, short for the ghargun, and then it hisses up a salty spray and descends into the deeps with its babies in tow.

In seconds, all that's left behind are ripples and the girl's empty body floating face-down in the water, bobbing slowly.

The old bitterness twists in his gut. He fights it down, taking the cold hook from around his throat and using it to reach for the corpse.

"Careful with that!"

The dead girl hugs herself as he fishes her body out of the water.

"You understand now?"

"The thing that bit me... why would you help them?"

The man sighs and leans on his hook. "If the babies you were hosting hatched back on Batua, the mother would've followed their call, sure as the sun rises. That's happened before, a long time ago. It's not gonna happen again."

He sets the dripping corpse-hook firmly back in place around his neck. The girl opens her mouth as if to talk, and then closes it, brow furrowed.

The morguist returns to his seat and begins rowing once more, this time back towards Batua.

"I'll take you home now, so your body will be properly taken care of. You'll be shriven and pass on from this world into the Great Current," he says. "That's what you want, isn't it?"

The girl frowns and then nods.

He looks out at the endless waters, knowing she doesn't consider herself lucky. There are worse fates.

She sits beside her corpse, trying not to look at it as the hoots of ancient, nameless ghosts echo across the water.

They row home together, a speck on the surface of the deep, dark sea. Toward the twinkling lights, where a mother waits.

THE OTHER FORTY-TWO

After a thousand years frozen between thoughts, Heart wakes to another dead system.

It wasn't always dead. The planets have been extensively mined and parked in an orbital synchrony that might last a billion years. The sun is surrounded by lenses casting complex beams and sheets of light out into the void. (These refractions were what drew Heart here.) There is biological life in abundance and evidence of advanced warfare.

The civilisation that once ruled here, however, is long gone.

Instead of feeling despair, Heart begins the long process of cataloguing her find. She is an expert archaeologist, as well as a capable explorer: those two skill sets are a rare combination. A seeker of knowledge on the edge of the known universe, the data she carries will be of great interest when she returns home.

On an icy moon among the system's outer planets, she finds something odd: an impossible configuration of matter in which electrons appear to be frozen. It looks like a monument of some kind, but under closer examination, she discovers that those electrons are indeed moving, only very, very slowly. The configuration is a sphere fifty thousand kilometres across, sustained by means unknown.

Clearly a machine. But for what purpose Heart can only guess.

It is the forty-second such machine she has found in her long travels.

They are not all like this one—complex coils of superconducting cables winding around each other in a knot so dense it risks collapsing into another kind of matter entirely.

One is a network of black holes orbiting in a deliberate dance that has lasted five billion years and shows no signs of ending.

A second is a series of continent-sized curved plates slipping and sliding over each in a clearly artificial process over which an entire biosphere has slowly accrued.

A third is a complex fold in space, invisible until entered, that contains subtle shifts in the universe's fundamental constants, shifts that come and go in ways that bear no relation to what lays outside.

Forty-two such devices are known to Heart. Taken as a set, they are superficially very different—yet they share two critical qualities.

One, they are very old.

Two, they are still operating.

Heart studies them while at the same taking care not to disturb them, or to get too close. She hasn't survived this long by recklessly assuming that the third characteristic they appear to share—that of ignoring her completely—will hold every time.

Still, she does her best to provoke a response, by signalling her origin, her species, her name, and her purpose. Not once did any of the previous forty-one respond, and this new one is no different. They just keep on churning or spinning or exploiting whatever particular kink of physics it is they depend on for their existence, waiting out eternity in slow, patient activity.

They haunt her, these remnants, these living mausoleums. What are they for? The building of them took great effort. Great returns must have been expected. Sometimes she imagines that there are living beings inside—the apotheoses of their civilisations, perhaps the ultimate embodiment of their creators themselves. If so, these machines might contain the greatest minds in the universe, wending away aeons in contemplation... of what? What are they thinking about? What can possibly require such an enormous expenditure of cognition?

Heart doesn't know. All she can do is continue her work in anticipation of the archaeologist's reward: to return home and properly examine her discoveries. Her life's labour won't be complete until she fully understands what she has found. She is looking forward to getting started.

Cracking the secrets of the ancients, Heart suspects, is going to take a great deal of thought.

SYNECDOCHE

There was an irony to them meeting like this — one the prisoner, the other the guard — but in jail as in all arenas, hope defies boundaries.

It began with an escapee from the world into their maze of bars and stone, a robin that found, among the boundaries and privations, a kinship with the captive men, who sought its favours as only those without freedom can seek anything that smacks of it. They sang to it. They offered stale crumbs saved from their morning meal in exchange for a brief perch on their outstretched finger. They cursed when it favoured other attempts to capture its companionship.

Only Quinn the guard knew of its humble origins, smuggled into the jail with a recent inmate, contraband that hatched before whatever fate its original owner had planned could befall it.

"A lucky escape for the bird," Quinn told the murderer Harley, with whom he had become conversational of late. "You don't want to know the details."

"S'pose you're right. T'was details got me in here."

"And details will get you out too. Has that new defence lawyer called on you yet?"

"Any day now."

The bird lifted its head in song, and all seemed good.

Until the warden learned of it and ordered the creature exterminated.

Capture proved difficult, thanks to its nimbleness and the many who would abet the bird in its bids for liberty. In the end, it came down to gas. The very medium that gave the robin flight took away its life.

Harley watched from behind bars, past Harley's broad shoulder, as the tiny corpse was removed. Where joy had been was now loss, and his heart, which had been filled with soaring hope, now lay heavy in his chest.

Seeing tears on Harley's cheeks, Quinn reached behind his back. Reached through the bars. Reached for Harley's large, leathered hand.

The sound of the bird going into the bin was drowned out by the pulse of two worn lives beating in time.

TALL TALES ABOUT TODAY MY
GREAT-GREAT-GRANDDAUGHTER
WILL TELL

Once upon a time, people used to fly about in Air-O-Planes. One day the people driving the Air-O-Plane fell asleep, and it crashed into a mountain. Everyone died.

When my great-great-grandma was young, people worked in places called "factories". They built things with their hands. But their hands were always getting caught in the machines and the machines were dirty and stupid and made everyone sick. Lots of people died. It was sad.

There was dirt *everywhere*. It piled up in huge mountains the Air-O-Planes crashed into. The rubbish fell into the ocean and made fish die. Birds would eat plastic and die, too. Great-great-grandpa cried when the whales went right down deep and never came back up.

Great-great-grandma had a car that was made by people's hands. It had a fire inside it that turned the wheels. The fire came from a tank she kept under the back seat. It was a kind of bomb. That's what Great-great-grandma calls it: an *old bomb*. She drove around for years with that old bomb before she gave the car to someone else. The other lady swapped her pieces of paper for it. The pieces of paper had numbers on them. They were called *money*. They didn't blow up, like cars sometimes did, so Great-great-grandma got a good deal.

I saw money once, in a museum.

Cars took people to the factories. The fire in the cars made lots of smoke, and the smoke going up made the sky heavy. The heavy sky made everything so hot underneath that the Air-O-Planes couldn't fly. More birds died. More people were sad. When the heat made all the ice melt, there was too much water everywhere. The fire in the cars went out. Some of the sad people got angry.

Great-great-grandma was angry at her parents. They shouldn't have built so many factories and cars, she says. Great-great-grandpa was angry too. He dreamed of getting rid of all the old bombs. He wanted the rubbish to go away and the whales to come back.

It's sad he didn't live long enough to see the sky get light again. He would've liked our new machines. They're much smarter than the old ones. Great-great-grandma says he died in the War, but I don't know what that is.

I'd like to fly in an Air-O-Plane, as long as it doesn't crash.

THE RISE AND FALL OF NEOLOGOPOLIS

simbiotic neuroplasm
psychotastic infogasm
socioscopic yottaphytes
—retrophobic trilobytes

THE WINTER GARDENER

A fine day down here means sky like a baby-blue bowl blurring into the horizon in all directions and no wind to speak of. Six degrees below freezing.

Cass heads inside to tend her garden.

Six months ago, the hydroponics shed was entirely covered in white. That thought is never far from her mind. Cold doesn't frighten her, and neither does the dark. But she loves plants like some people love cats, indiscriminately and with great fervour.

There are no trees native to Antarctica. No bushes. No grass, even. Just rocks and snow and the odd patch of hardy moss.

She pulls open the external door and slams it shut behind her, tugging off her boots and gloves with the same determination that she attempts to cast aside her misgivings. It seems petty to focus on the fate of two guys hauled out of a ruined American base at the beginning of summer. But she does.

Frozen to death, she heard. Maybe still alive, she also heard. The lack of a clear answer troubles her. In Antarctica, everyone's in it together. There is no room for ambiguity on that point. So what was the big secret?

Through the internal door, she reaches for a paint brush with one hand, spray bottle with the other and begins her usual, calming ritual. Fertilizing with the brush, watering with the other. She's the proud farmer of numerous tomatoes, chillies and zucchinis, a veritable forest of herbs and salad greens, and many dozens of seedlings just beginning to sprout.

Nothing bothers her in here, behind two closed doors.

Until she hears the railgun fire down by the wharf, the powerful whine-crack, whine-crack of two quick shots.

She freezes in mid brush, then jumps as someone bangs on the shed wall.

"Come see, Cass. It's the biggest yet!"

She doesn't want to see, but she has to. They're all in it together. With shaking hands, she puts down her gardening tools, tugs boots and gloves back on, and braces herself for the outside.

Where it's still sunny and still cold, but the still air is now broken by shouting down near the water. There's a roaring, hissing sound too, and the whine of the jerry-rigged weapon charging again. She hurries towards the source of the sounds, careful not to slip on patches of ice. She can't afford a broken limb now there's nowhere left to be airlifted to.

A dozen of her fellow expeditioners are gathered at the wharf, half of them ready by the chemical tubs containing potent mixtures from the Dangerous Goods Store. If anything gets too close, the tubs will be tipped into the water and their contents set ablaze. This has worked before.

She's nervous because she can't see what Ronnie, the guy who banged on her door, is pointing at. He's a long-limbed, hipster tradie in boots, shorts and cold-weather jacket. Cass is too short, the angle not quite right, as it wasn't the one night they'd hooked up after she asked him to show her how to use the oxy-acetylene welder.

Then the roaring hiss recurs. Something vast rolls onto its back in the black water and flails its many-coloured tentacles. *Those* she can see. Or are they many-hinged legs? Perhaps antennae? At this distance, it's hard to tell.

Flesh. Alien, deadly.

Whine-crack. Tissue bursts in the creature's side. Whine-crack. Again.

The thing howls and goes under.

Cass hugs herself, waiting, but it doesn't reappear a second time.

"You see it?" asks Ronnie, practically dancing with adrenaline. "You see that?"

"I saw enough." She turns and heads back up the hill.

"They're getting bigger!"

"I know."

Small comfort, this understanding that things are getting worse.

Up north, when the outbreaks took hold, "flesh flooding" some dark wit called it. Everything living rolled up into a monstrous tide of tentacles and teeth, devouring every other living thing in its path. Plants and animals alike.

Not here, where there's little biomass outside the ocean. The cold too, seems to slow the alien growth, maybe even stop it. Some have suggested that the ice is where it came from—something defrosted as tundra turned to slush or dug out of the permafrost. And now the creatures boiling out of the Southern Ocean are getting bigger, and the change in season can't come soon enough...

It's ironic. In Cass's former life, she wondered if she'd live to see the day when summer overtook winter as the most feared season—blasting hot, plants dying in waterless deserts, melanoma rampant...

Those two American guys are the lucky ones, she sometimes thinks. They didn't live to see this summer.

She retreats to her garden and wills her hands to stop shaking. It's safe here, she tells herself. Safe as houses. Last week, three plant operators plus a cadre of plumbers and electricians joined two containers up to the original hydroponics shed, thus tripling its capacity. One of the boffins is coaxing dried beans back to life. Her plants could one day support the entire station, or at least take the pressure off the tinned stores now there'll be no resupplies. That's the plan, although it could change next time the creatures in the ocean come too close. Or the time after that.

We're all in it together, she whispers to her charges.

Cass has the will, and the welder, to protect the last garden on Earth.

IMMATERIAL PROGRESS

"With this advance in transportation, humanity's conquest of space is complete. I am profoundly moved."

Year 1

Interviewer: "Thank you for joining us, Professor Joosten."

Joosten: "My pleasure."

Interviewer: "One year has passed since your historic voyage by dematerialization from Beijing to Boston. How are your memories of that day?"

Joosten: "They're permanently etched on my brain, Stephen."

Interviewer: "Do you recall what you had for breakfast that morning."

Joosten: "No... no, that I do not remember. Next question?"

Year 2

Gossgasm:

> "Sources close to the Hanuman Project inform us that the rumored illness suffered by Professor Joosten directly after her journey through the d-mat device was caused by contaminated eggs, and is in no way connected to the process itself. The rest of her breakfast that morning, we are told, consisted of bread, bacon, and a strong cup of coffee."

Year 4

Q: "Speculation regarding a leaked recording of events in the receiving chamber just will not die away. Would you care to comment, Professor Joosten?"

A: "No, I would not."

Q: "Is it true that you were violently ill immediately upon arrival?"

A: "Of course it's not true! These are lies spread by critics and competitors, and they have no basis in reality whatsoever!"

Year 8

Full transcript from the Boston Chamber:

> "With this advance in transportation, humanity's conquest of space is complete. I am profoundly moved and ... uh, excuse me ... uh, I think I'm going to be—" (*vomits*)

Year 16

World Holistic Leadership propaganda leaflet:

"They SAY it was just motion sickness. They SAY they lied only to stop wrong ideas from getting into our heads. Well, I say the only source of wrong ideas around here is the Hanuman Project itself. What other secrets have they got hidden in their Frankenstein laboratories? How many other leaked recordings are yet to come out? D-mat is killing you. Wake up and smell the bacon!"

Year 32

Sable, 16: "Did you hear about the first person who ever used d-mat?"

Rudy, 16: "Yeah, she had ham and eggs for breakfast, and when she arrived she had a stomach ache that just got worse and worse and worse. Eventually they opened her up, and found a dead chick and a baby pig, trying to get out."

Aisling, 17: "Piglet, you idiot. What a load of rubbish. That could never happen."

Sroy, 15: "But imagine if it *did* ..."

Year 64

Newsthread:

"Today marks the death at 108 of Jenaya Joosten, earliest adopter of a technological innovation that transformed the world. Longtime advocate of alternate uses of d-mat, particularly in the fields of reclamation and medicine, she was never able to shake allegations of conspiracy and cover-ups that dogged her career and personal life (the novelty song 'Joosten, We Have A Problem' has enjoyed a resurgence in popularity). Professor Joosten will be publically mourned by her family and colleagues in London this Tuesday."

Year 128

"Once upon a time, people traveled through space. Now, thanks to warp drive technology, *space* comes to *us*. Where's that bucket, Prof Joosten? Just kidding."

CAPTAIN ZEPHYRIAH SAROFF, ON THE SAFE
ARRIVAL OF ANDROMEDA SPACEWAYS TEST
VEHICLE *ALCUBIERRE III.*

NEW SONGS FOR KATE

Marcie has a good ear and a fine voice. That's the only thing that kept her alive all these years. Three decades she has staved off starvation by performing the tunes she knows best, moving when the crops fail or the mood turns sour, as so often it seems to for no reason at all.

People enjoy her show, and not just the folk who remember the old days. Just lately she's been building a reputation among the kids, such as those she's playing to now in Brooklyn. Word spreads as fast as horses run, which is nothing compared to electricity and internet, but as there's nothing else faster that's fine.

"Kate Bush was the greatest singer who ever lived," Marcie addresses hundreds of bright-eyed teenagers while the echoes of "Babooshka" fade away. They like songs that tell stories full of drama. They like legends, and she's happy to provide. "Here's one of my personal favourites."

The crowd sways in time to the opening chords of Adele's "Rolling in the Deep", knowing no better and not needing to. Legends don't have to be accurate. Legends simplify. Legends keep Marcie fed.

THE DARK MATTERS

The one thing she cannot think is that she's crazy.

Susan Barker is a small teenager with brown hair. Her weight is within the healthy band, and when she talks her eyes are still. When her therapist responds, however, her gaze moves constantly, roving around the office as though looking for something.

"They live in the shadows," she says. "They come out at night."

"Why?"

"Which part?"

"Let's start with the shadows."

"They can't stand the light because they're fragile. They're all that's left of us when the matter is gone."

Her eyes skitter about as her therapist takes this in.

"If I turned out the lights now, would they come?"

"No, because you're here. They like it when I'm alone."

"What do they do when you're alone?"

"Nothing but press in real close, all around me. I can feel them. It's like the darkness has weight, although I know that's impossible. They don't have any weight. They're just..."

"Ghosts?"

"No. That's not the right word. They're... echoes... of all the versions of me who went into a d-mat booth and didn't come out the other end."

The therapist taps the tips of his fingers together. The reference to d-mat ghosts is unexpected. Ever since the invention of matter transmission there have been people afraid of being disintegrated. They talk of zombies, of souls ascending to heaven long before the physical body has grown old and died, of half-remembered screams as the lasers go to work...

"Not just me, other people, too," Susan goes on. "Sometimes I can feel my mother next to me, and my ex-boyfriend on top of me. They come because they know me."

"Why?"

"Just because, I guess. Look, I know what you're going to tell me. You're going to tell me I'm wrong. But I know I'm not wrong. Life is complexity—that's what I learned in biology—but what difference does it make if complexity is born or grown or made out of nothing? As soon as someone steps from a booth, they have a new soul to replace the one in their old body. And meanwhile the old soul is set free. The old soul can wander for years before it gets home, where of course there's no room for it anymore. So it just... sticks close... remembering who it was and not feeling bad about it, I guess. It rejoices in me. It loves me, and so do all the others."

"That's an interesting theory, Susan."

"If you don't believe me, that's okay. I know I'm right. And if you put me on drugs like my parents want, that's fine too. You can even lock me away. It won't make any difference. They'll find me again. We'll always be together. Just so long as you turn the lights out sometimes, they'll come."

The therapist nods, even though she is wrong.

That wasn't what he was going to say at all.

The one thing I cannot admit is that she's right.

Not about the source of the dark ones, although her theory haunts me through the following sessions, and haunts me still when I get home, where I close the windows carefully, ensuring that no glimmer can enter my chambers and halls. I turn out the lights. The darkness is perfect. Through long practice I have learned to navigate without use of my eyes. I feel my way through dinner and toilet, never fumbling, never stumbling, all my other senses heightened.

I sense them gathering like soft breaths of night. They know my routine. As I lay down to sleep they press in around me, touching me everywhere—my cheeks, my eyelids, my throat, my stomach, my scrotum, the soles of my feet. So often mistaken for puffs of air, they are present even here in the blackened stillness of my room, where there can be no breezes.

Susan was right. There are things that live in the night. And she is not the only one who feels them.

The first patient to come to me with this complaint was a physicist. He explained the sensation away by evoking neutrinos that sluice constantly through us, unseen and unfelt. Why shouldn't some of them stick and form negative images of us, particularly when we ourselves, as users of d-mat, spend so much of our lives as incorporeal energies?

Then there was the social scientist who evoked impressions cast in a collective consciousness, psychic eddies that survive much longer and travel much further than they would have in times before d-mat.

A biologist thought it was the forgotten flora that inhabits our bodies—on our skin and in our guts—that lingers when we have moved on, like the skeleton of a leaf when the rest has crumbled away. So similar to Susan's metaphor.

I know that they are the memories of my past selves, the ghosts of lost emotions, saved by d-mat from forgetfulness in the memory of the universe. Therefore I do not fear sickening and wasting away as some of my more superstitious patients have. I wish only to keep my dark ones close and bask in their affinity.

Shadows press in around me. I open my arms in welcome.

The one thing you can be sure of is that we've always been here.

Sometimes you have banished us unknowingly, with your electric light and your cities. Sometimes you welcome us back, as in this world of plenty, where technologies powerful enough to manipulate matter at its basest level allow everyone the luxury of a darkened bedroom.

We are here, waiting for the lights to go out. Desiring you. Loving you. Hungering for you.

We come from the shadows to whisper sweet nothings.

We come to feed.

LOOPHOLES IN LIGHT

"Hello, Andre. How nice to see you again. I knew I would, one day."

"I... can't say the feeling is mutual, Doctor Pedersen. It's amazing you're still alive!"

"Not a day goes by I don't thank the miracle that is modern science. But miracles can be misused... and so here we are. I'm sure you are aware that the law has not changed—"

"I am indeed. D-mat cannot be used for the purpose of suicide, because matter transmitters are not death machines—although of course they are, no matter what the state says. They strip everyone who uses them back to their component atoms, killing them in the process. To deny oblivion to those who desire it is—"

"A mercy, not a cruelty. I know you disagree, Andre."

"Of course I do. I wish to die just as dearly as other people wish to visit Mount Everest or the moon. Their wishes are granted. Why not mine?"

"Because you lack the clinical criteria for legal euthanasia—unless you now claim to be depressed, terminally ill or infirm... ?"

"You can see in my file that I'm none of those things. You can tell by looking at me."

"Yet you tried again, knowing that you would end up here, in the Recovery Room, with me or someone like me?"

"Being counseled as I have been counseled many times before? Yes, I did."

"Why, Andre?"

"Because this time is different. This time... I came to say goodbye."

"Don't tell me you have changed your mind!"

"That will never happen, Doctor Pedersen. On the contrary, I will change your mind."

"Ah, this is why you smile. Proceed, then. If you have spent the last four decades devising an argument, you have my full attention."

"I have done nothing of the sort. My plan was formed when last we met. You suggested I take up tourism instead of dying. Do you remember?"

"My memory... is not what it used to be, but yes, I saw that remark in your files while awaiting completion of the Recovery process."

"Well, I took your advice to heart. I did travel. Around the world first, then across the solar system—and what a fascinating place that turned out to be. Almost the resolve to end my life fled, but I remain as certain as ever that continuing my existence is futile. To commit suicide via d-mat is my wish, once the state no longer stands in my way."

"I fear, Andre, that the state will never accede to your fetishistic wish—"

"But it must, and so must you. You see, I didn't just travel across the solar system to visit the planets—Jupiter in her ribbons and Saturn's bejeweled hat! I extended my journey far beyond the pool of light surrounding our sun, to the Plutonians, to the comets, to the edge of utter darkness itself. Once I stood on a rock that was closer to a neighboring sun than it is to our own, feeling the glorious crunch of eons-old air-ice under my insulated boots, and... Oh, I must stop lest I give you false hope! Amid all this beautiful strangeness and wonder, how could I not feel anything but jaded, and more certain than ever that my final wish will be attained, today."

"Travel may have broadened your mind, but I fail to see how it will alter mine."

"Consider, good doctor, that a person's existence is measured in moments. An hour here, a year there, all adding up to a lifetime. What happens when the flow of these moments is interrupted? We call this death: the measurement is complete; the addition comes to a full stop.

"Yet if the flow is restored... via d-mat say... then a miracle occurs! Life is restored, the count continues once more. The moments of death between life and life renewed are... inconvenient... and ignored.

"Imagine what happens as one travels to the stars via d-mat. When the body is torn asunder to release its precious data, data that is captured, frozen, and stored, this precious cargo is encoded bit by bit into a beam of twisted laser light, which fires outward into space at a precisely defined speed—the speed of light itself. There a person remains, unchanging, unliving... by any practical definition, dead.

"That packet of data might travel many years before reaching the receiver and being returned to matter. Years of death-debt, which a few days of sight-seeing cannot counterbalance."

"That is one way of—"

"Let me finish my spiel, Doctor Pedersen. I have rehearsed many times! What happens when the sum of one's living days are outnumbered by those spent trapped in d-mat's deadly thrall? How can one possibly be considered alive when for most of one's existence one has been precisely the opposite?

"If you do the math, Doctor, you will find that, thanks to my interstellar adventures, I have now passed that critical juncture. I'm now more dead than alive, historically speaking, and you cannot therefore, in good faith, deny me the wish to return to my proper state. One of nonexistence, in the eyes of all but the most pedantic."

"Ah, but the state *is* pedantic, Andre! This is a detail you appear to have overlooked in your ruminations: the fundamental difference between someone who has been scanned and stored and someone who has been scanned and erased. The former remains living by every legal definition; the latter has died, either by their own hand or by someone else's. Whether someone has been stored for the majority of the time since their birth is irrelevant. They *have* been stored. That is the critical thing."

"I'm glad you feel that way, Doctor Pedersen."

"You are?"

"Yes."

"Would you care to explain why?"

"Can you not guess? I do not ask to be erased, but to be returned to nonexistence, a state that only I, the pedant in this scenario, might care to distinguish from true death."

"I begin to see now... Yes... Let me say, Andre, how much I admire your dedication—no, that is too mild a word. To have pursued this goal for so many years, without pause or distraction—"

"Don't credit me with too much. For me it has been but a matter of weeks."

"Regardless, to fling yourself with such will into an unknowable future... You have risen vastly in my regard. It has been such a pleasure conversing with you."

"So you will grant me my heart's desire?"

"Yes. The state cannot stop you from *travelling*. May I ask where you intend to go?"

"The Andromeda galaxy. The journey of my data will take two and half million years."

"And naturally you do not expect a receiver to overtake you, in which case your signal, stored in the very fabric of the universe, would overshoot and vanish into the void forever... A gamble, then, and a bold one. I eagerly await the result."

"You? Doctor Pedersen, as well preserved as you are, surely you cannot expect to live long enough to find out!"

"I can be sure of it—although some would quibble over the definition of what it means to *live*. My physical body died many years ago, but my d-mat pattern is reactivated whenever I am needed in the Recovery Room. Isn't that remarkable, how our destinies have converged?"

"Please, don't tell me—"

"Yes, Andre, when humanity devises a way to surpass that twisted light beam containing your data, I will be there to greet you in Andromeda, all those years hence. And I for one eagerly await our conversation."

A BETTER PLACE

Pop goes the cork, momentarily stilling the dawn chorus, and I am filled with the sense that what we are doing in the cemetery is slightly profane. My mother, my sister Cass and I on a picnic rug at the foot of Dad's grave. Thank God we brought sparkling wine, not a heavy red.

"Don't ever think you're too good for this world," Mum says, raising her empty glass to be filled with a blush that perfectly matches both the lightening sky and the skin around her eyes, "because you've probably got it the wrong way around. That's what your Dad used to say."

"Well, cheers," says Cass with a determined tone, and we dutifully clink and sip. Bubbles go up my nose, provoking the tears that I have been holding back all the way here.

"I miss him." In my voice, the child I thought I'd long outgrown. I turn away from them, seeing through a watery veil the rows of memorials, each a rose bush raising handfuls of white petals to the sky. The marker at the foot of Dad's reads "For the health and prompt release of asylum seekers. *Gratis enim vita tua,* Dennis Wright."

"I wish he was still here," I say.

"And what if he'd been hit by a car?" Cass responds. "Or got cancer? What would've been the point of that?"

"Please don't argue, not today," Mum cautions us. "He wanted to help people. It would've been wrong to stop him."

I wipe my eyes. The birdsongs are returning, as I suppose they must. Life goes on, not caring that Dennis Wright has been gone a whole year.

The roses. I had forgotten them. The most impressive thing about the cemetery is how many memorials there are, row after row, hundreds upon hundreds, stretching as far as the eye can see.

So many do-gooders, I think. *Imagine how terrible the world would be without them.*

My heart lightens as the sun crests the hills to the east. A new breath fills my chest.

"Has Sam heard from the Mission Board?" Mum changes the subject.

My sister looks uneasy, her focus on Dad's death rocked by this intrusion from the real world. "Yes. The email came yesterday."

"Does that mean you'll be leaving?"

"In the next two months. We don't know exactly when."

"Well, congratulations. That's wonderful news. I'm really happy for you."

"I didn't want to tell you because…"

"Honey, I understand. Your father would be pleased, too. Perhaps he made this happen—you know, one last gift to us all."

Mum raises her glass and we clink again. I can hear the ache in her voice, but Cass doesn't. My sister beams at the thought that Dad played a part in her future happiness. I beam back at her. Perhaps it's true. It's not my place to tarnish what he so bravely did, with words or tears, both of which I fear will be too liquid ever to entirely quell.

Some nights I imagine the priests opening the vein and wonder what they said to him as his life ebbed away, whether he thought of us one last time or if he focused instead on those who would benefit from his gift. He never met them, and never would, but he believed in them with a fierceness, a fierceness that seemed almost like ferocity when I asked him once if he was *completely* sure that this was what he wanted, if he had no thoughts at all that maybe, just maybe, he could do *more* by staying here, with us, with the ones who loved him most.

"There is no measuring the good in this world," he told me the last time we spoke. "It multiplies endlessly. But don't ever be fooled into thinking that it comes without sacrifice."

There's that word. It sits on my tongue, tasting today of sparkling rosé, not ashes and loss.

"Well done, Dad," I say, thinking of that line from the Bible, *Do this in remembrance of me*, and we clink glasses a third time to seal the charm. We bourgeois, we favoured, we bereft, we fatherless, we blessed by the good man who departed the world in hope of making it better.

PREVIOUS PUBLICATIONS

Some stories in this collection have been previously published, sometimes in very different forms.

Sean Williams was born in the dry, flat lands of South Australia, where he still lives with his wife and family and teaches creative writing at Flinders University. He has been called many things in his time, including (somewhat ostentatiously) "the premier Australian speculative fiction writer of the age" (Aurealis), the "Emperor of Sci-Fi" (Adelaide Advertiser), the "Lord of the Genre" (Perth Writers' Festival), and the "King of Chameleons" (Australian Book Review) for the diversity of his published output. That output includes fifty novels for readers all ages, over one hundred short stories across numerous genres, the odd published poem, and even a sci-fi musical. He is a multiple recipient of the Aurealis and Ditmar Awards and has been nominated for the Philip K. Dick Award, the Seiun Award, the NSW Premier's Awards, and the William Atheling Jr. Award for criticism. He received the "SA Great" Literature Award in 2000 and the Peter McNamara Award for contributions to Australian speculative fiction in 2008. His latest novels are *Impossible Music* and *Her Perilous Mansion*, both Childrens Book Council of Australian Notable Books.

facebook.com/seanwilliamsauthor
twitter.com/adelaidesean
instagram.com/adelaidesean
amazon.com/Sean-Williams

ALSO BY SEAN WILLIAMS

Series

The Books of the Change

The Books of the Cataclysm

The Broken Land

Astropolis

Twinmaker

The Fixers

Star Wars: The Force Unleashed

Troubletwisters (with Garth Nix)

Have Sword, Will Travel (with Garth Nix)

Evergence (with Shane Dix)

Orphans (with Shane Dix)

Geodesica (with Shane Dix)

Star Wars: New Jedi Order: Force Heretic (with Shane Dix)

Standalone novels

Metal Fatigue

The Resurrected Man

Her Perilous Mansion

Spirit Animals: Blood Ties (with Garth Nix)

Star Wars: The Old Republic: Fatal Alliance